ideals®
HOME

Vol. 48, No. 5

Publisher, Patricia A. Pingry
Editor, Nancy J. Skarmeas
Art Director, Patrick McRae
Contributing Editors, Marty Sowder Brooks, Lansing Christman, Deana Deck, Russ Flint, Carol Shaw Johnston, Pamela Kennedy
Editorial Assistant, LaNita Kirby

ISBN 0-8249-1092-3

IDEALS—Vol. 48, No. 5 August MCMXCI IDEALS (ISSN 0019-137X) is published eight times a year: February, March, May, June, August, September, November, December by IDEALS PUBLISHING CORPORATION, P.O. Box 148000, Nashville, Tenn. 37214. Second-class postage paid at Nashville, Tennessee, and additional mailing offices. Copyright © MCMXCI by IDEALS PUB-LISHING CORPORATION. POSTMASTER: Send address changes to Ideals, Post Office Box 148000, Nashville, Tenn. 37214-8000. All rights reserved. Title IDEALS registered U.S. Patent Office.

SINGLE ISSUE—$4.95
ONE-YEAR SUBSCRIPTION—eight consecutive issues as published—$19.95
TWO-YEAR SUBSCRIPTION—sixteen consecutive issues as published—$35.95
Outside U.S.A., add $6.00 per subscription year for postage and handling.

ACKNOWLEDGMENTS

OLD TOWNS from *REVERIE* by Josephine Powell Beaty: Used by permission. HOMECOMING from *SUNDIAL OF THE SEASONS*. Copyright © 1964 by Hal Borland. Reprinted by permission of Francis Collin, Literary Agent. THE CHARM OF AN OLD HOUSE from HEARTH-FIRE by Marel Brown: Used by permission of the author. SO LONG AS THERE ARE HOMES from the *LIGHT OF THE YEARS* by Grace Noll Crowell. Copyright © 1963 by Grace Noll Crowell. Reprinted by permission of HarperCollinsPublishers. OUR HOUSE from *HARBOR LIGHTS OF HOME* by Edgar A. Guest. Copyright © 1928 by Reilly & Lee Company: Used by permission of the estate. HOME-LOVING HEARTS by Edna Jaques from *MY KITCHEN WINDOW*: Copyright © 1941 in Canada by Thomas Allen & Son Limited. Used by permission. SEA SPELL by Rose Koralewsky from *NEW ENGLAND HERITAGE AND OTHER POEMS*: Copyright © 1949 by Bruce Humphries, Inc. Used by permission of Branden Publishing Company. ENDURING THINGS from ROADS WIDE WITH WONDER by Mary E. Linton: Used by permission of the author. HOME from *MOMENTS OF ETERNITY* by Betty W. Stoffel. Copyright 1954: Used by permission of the author. THE HOUSE WITH MANY WINDOWS from the book *GOLDEN HOURS* by Patience Strong: Used by permission of Rupert Crew Limited. HOME from POEMS FROM MY HEART by Phyllis Michael. Copyright © 1964 by Phyllis Michael. Used by permission. Our special thanks to the following whose addresses we were unable to locate: Annabelle Attwater for HOUSES; Mildred Morris Gilbert for COUNTERPART; Mrs. Robert Glidden for MY HOME; Eloise Hamilton for EARTH, MY VILLAGE; Elizabeth Olsen for THE OPEN DOOR; and Geraldine Ross for BIDE AT HOME.

Four-color separations by Rayson Films, Inc., Waukesha, Wisconsin

Printing by The Banta Company, Menasha, Wisconsin

The paper used in this publication meets the minimum requirements of American National Standard for Information Sciences—Permanence of Paper for Printed Library Materials, ANSI Z39.48-1984.

Unsolicited manuscripts will not be returned without a self-addressed stamped envelope.

Inside Covers
Richard Hook

HOME

Betty W. Stoffel

If you have known a home that daily weaves
Its patterned happiness through those who share,
If you have known a home where loving leaves
Its spirit of contentment on the air,
If home has meant the haven of all peace,
The resting place of heart's security,
The sum of every joy, the soul's increase,
The total of all good life meant to be,

Then you can be assured that home above
Will be more sweet than all your memories here;
For those who know a home of earthly love
Will only find the heavenly love more dear.
It matters not what kind of house or where,
So long as those we love are living there.

Home-Loving Hearts

Edna Jaques

Home-loving hearts have all that makes life good
Safe in the shelter of their kindly roof,
Kinship and love and gracious motherhood—
These are of life the very warp and woof,
The silver strands that keep the world in place,
The age-old knitted fibre of the race.

Home-loving hearts have little plots of ground,
The ancient kindly earth to nurture them,
The sun to make small pools of fleeting gold,
The starry sky to be a diadem,
Quiet old streets where neighbors come and go,
Old lamps that have a friendly yellow glow.

Home-loving hearts that never learn to stray
From simple tender joys of home and hearth,
Who tread the worn old paths of common folk,
Feel the warm throbbing of the ancient earth.
Life is so kind to them who keep her ways,
Crowning with peace the evening of their days.

Photo Opposite
THE PATIO
Sigrid Owen
International Stock Photography

Our Little Town

Seventy-five years beside the sea
This village nestled there—
Snug and content with the easy life
And friendships beyond compare.
Relaxation, lolling on the beach,
Sport fishing from the pier;
Sheer joy strolling along the strand
Greeting friends and strangers everywhere.
Riding the waves as they roll in
To take command of the beach;
Picking up shells as the tide goes out,
Feeling the sand shift beneath your feet.

The sun hangs low on the horizon—
Come join the folks on promenade
Gathered to watch the setting sun
And witness the close of day.
Night drops the curtain on the sunset,
The moon now lights the stage
And millions of stars shine on the water
Bobbing and reflecting from the waves.

There's no place like the beach at sunset—
Or like the moonlit waves of gold—
Or like the tranquil beach at sunrise
When colored mists unfold.
Seventy-five years is but a short day
When eternity is our goal,
May our little town retain its charm
Forever, as the centuries unfold.

Mildred C. Sprouse
Seal Beach, California

Reflections

Coming Home

As I look from my kitchen window
At the old pine tree in the yard
I marvel he stands so stately,
Like the changing of the guard.

There's a beaten old swing hanging
From his massive protective arm;
For years he's sheltered many
And kept them free from harm.

I remember the running and shouting
And some raucous little fights,
As my children put forth efforts
To establish childhood rights.

The rope on the swing is frazzled
And the seat has warped a bit . . .
Then I realize there are things to do—
I don't have time to sit.

So I drag out the old ladder
And hang a brand new rope,
For I know there'll soon be laughter
And my heart leaps high with hope.

Today they're coming home again
With little ones of their own;
That swing will nearly reach the sky
And that old pine tree will groan.

It seems a hundred years they've been
So far away from me,
But now they'll fill this house again
And set my heartaches free.

Florence Cantwell
Middleton, Wisconsin

Home

I do not strive to seek fortune or fame;
My dream is a house on a country lane;
A home filled with tenderness, warmth, and love,
A family blessed by his presence above.

The voices of children I do so love to hear,
These are the precious things that I hold dear.
Family get-togethers in this house I see,
And a garden, dear God, as a shrine to thee.

Eleanor Joan Kearney
Coram, New York

Common Blessings

Thomas Curtis Clark

Lord of my years, can life be bare
With beauty springing everywhere?
Can I forlorn and lonely be
With sweet birdsong in every tree?
Can I succumb to doubt and fear
With tasks to do and friends to cheer?
What matters it if I be poor
With roses blooming at my door?
My garden is a maze of gold
As summer hours their dreams unfold.
Can I complain, by sorrows pent,
Knowing I have the boon, content?
Trouble shall flee and fear take wing,
For life still brings me songs to sing.
Lord of my days, how thankful I
For a thankful heart, as life goes by.

DAY LILIES
Adam Jones, Photographer

The Commonplace

Georgia B. Adams

The day lilies are blooming now
   across the fields;
What a friendly atmosphere
   their scenery yields.

Along the highways and beside
   each wayward trail,
Banked on the slopes of brooks and streams,
   through hill and dale

DAY LILIES
Tyler, Texas
Gene Ahrens, Photographer

I see them curtsy in the breeze,
    as if to say
"Our loveliness is yours; we're glad
    you've come this way!"

Tomorrow, other blooms will take
    their place and then,

One day to live, they too will fall
    to earth again.

These common treasures of the dust
    life's byways grace,
And I thank God each day for
    the commonplace.

11

like very much

Come in
for
a Moment

Virginia Gilman

You're always welcome at my house,
Come in and hang your hat;
The tea is brewing on the stove,
We'll sit awhile and chat.

But if you can't look past the clutter
Or ignore the dusty floor,
You'll want to come another day
To call here at my door,

For yesterday my broom and dustpan
Never left their spot;
My dishes still lie in the sink
With dirty pans and pots.

You see, my children needed me
To share some joys and fears,
To bounce them gently on my knee
And wipe away their tears.

So last upon my busy list
Was sweeping up the dust,
For someday they'll no longer need
A mother's tender touch.

You're always welcome at my house,
Come in and hang your hat;
Just please remember love comes first
And housework's always last.

STONE WALL AND WISTERIA
Lefever/Grushow
Grant Heilman, Inc.

Photo Overleaf
CORN POPPIES BY ANCIENT WALL
M. Thonig
H. Armstrong Roberts

BIDE AT HOME

Geraldine Ross

Not only hearts that heed the pull
Of wanderlust are beautiful.
The rose is stained a deeper red
Through roots the same rich earth has fed.
Vines, tangled by long years, have won
Grape clusters, purpling in the sun.
A friendliness, a bond, is found
In knowing well a bit of ground;
There is wisdom in the will
That bends itself to being still.

Photo Opposite
ROSES AND FENCE
Dietrich Stock Photos, Inc.

COLLECTOR'S CORNER

Dollhouses

A dollhouse mansion, 1890.

Two tiny dolls share a pot of tea.

Dollhouses are the stuff that dreams are made of—the dreams of children who imagine themselves grown-up, and the dreams of dollhouse collectors worldwide who find in their miniature houses an ideal domestic world.

Dollhouses and the miniatures that furnish them have fascinated people for centuries. Egyptian, Trojan, and Greek miniatures date back as far as 1900 B.C. Anthropologists believe that these miniatures were made both for the amusement of children and for religious and symbolic purposes. The first dollhouses were actually cabinets made to hold the collections of miniatures popular with early seventeenth-century European royalty. Until the late nineteenth century, dollhouses remained a hobby for the wealthy, but as general prosperity increased, the popularity of the

dollhouse spread. In today's market, a dollhouse can be bought and furnished on any budget, especially with the help of thrift stores, flea markets, and yard sales.

A vast assortment of dollhouses is available today, ranging from simple one-room box houses to elegantly furnished mansions with electric lights and running water. Collectors find enjoyment in building or restoring a dollhouse and then furnishing it with just the right assortment of miniatures. Some create small scale replicas of their own homes; others rely on memories of a favorite childhood home; still others create a dollhouse that is pure fantasy.

Scale is one of the most important considerations for dollhouse enthusiasts. Collectors can decide to collect one-twelfth or two-twelfth scale items. It is best to choose furnishings that are either antique or modern, metal or wood, working or non-working; although a variety can sometimes be pleasingly arranged, a group of unrelated objects can often be more trouble than it is worth.

There are many resources for collectors interested in dollhouses. Books, magazines, clubs, and newsletters all address the many facets of the hobby, and museums displaying collections exist in almost every state. But one great attraction of dollhouse decorating and collecting is that no special expertise is necessary; inside each of us is a picture of "home," whether real or imagined. This is the only prerequisite for the collector.

The dollhouse can be whatever its creator desires. Free from the complications and difficulties of everyday life—the dollhouse's floors never need sweeping and the dishes are always clean—the world of the dollhouse is simple and predictable. The inhabitants are always healthy and happy; the family is always together; the future is always full of promise. With a dollhouse, real world limitations do not apply.

Like a real home, the dollhouse is a wise investment; but the return is sentimental, not financial. None of us, certainly, would trade real life for the idealized world of the dollhouse. Nonetheless, the allure of the wonderful, miniature world of the dollhouse is timeless, and—to dollhouse collectors worldwide—irresistible.

Carol Shaw Johnston, a public school teacher, writes articles and short stories. She lives with her family in Brentwood, Tennessee.

The Tiffany-Platt House, mid-nineteenth century.

The South Jersey House, 1870.

Photos courtesy of the Washington Doll's House Museum, Washington, D.C.

The House with Many Windows

Patience Strong

A selfish life is like a house
    without a windowpane,
A house from which the eye can see
    no sunshine, no rain;
No outward view, no glimpse of heaven,
    only solid walls;
A house like a prison where
    no gleam of sunlight falls.

A selfless life is like a house
    with windows everywhere
From which the world is seen
    with all its joys and care;
Windows open to the winds
    of hope and sympathy,
Windows lit with shining lamps
    of faith and charity.

Photo Opposite
HOME IN SUMMER
Randolph Center, Vermont
Dietrich Stock Photos, Inc.

TRAVELER'S Diary

The White House: A Truly American Home

The White House is not simply the home of the President. Its rooms, its furniture, its paintings, its countless mementos make it a living story of the whole experience of the American people, the habits and the hopes, the triumphs and the troubles, and the bedrock faith of our Nation.

Lady Bird Johnson

For nearly two hundred years, American presidents and their families have made the White House their home. Each new family has left behind something of itself, from a particular taste in furniture to the inspirational image of a courageous leader. The result is a wonderful repository of political and domestic history—a truly American home.

The White House sits at the end of the wide thoroughfare of Pennsylvania Avenue. Its design is the work of Irish architect James Hoban, who modeled the residence after the Chateau de Rastignac in France and Leinster House in Dublin, Ireland, both of which drew on the Palladian architecture of mid-eighteenth century Europe.

John Adams was the first chief executive to occupy the presidential residence. He moved into the still-unfinished home on November 1, 1800. That night, with workmen's shanties surrounding his front door, the central staircase only a pile of timbers on the floor, and the autumn chill seeping through unfinished walls, John Adams saw beyond the chaos to the solemn promise of his new home at 1600 Pennsylvania Avenue. He wrote to his wife, Abigail, "I pray Heaven to bestow the best of Blessings on this House and all that shall hereafter inhabit it. May none but honest and wise Men ever rule under this roof." A century later, President Franklin Delano Roosevelt had these words carved into the mantel of the State Dining Room, preserving them for all future residents.

This pattern has been repeated ever since; history is created by one administration and preserved by another. The White House is constantly evolving, as each new president shapes his home and office. Thomas Jefferson, perhaps still annoyed at having his own design for the residence rejected, used his substantial clout as our third president to make significant alterations to the building's design. The British did some unwelcome remodeling of their own during the War of 1812. Their flames gutted the interior of the house and so discolored the exterior walls that the now distinctive coat of white paint was necessary to cover the smoke-blackened Virginia sandstone. President Truman also saw fit to do some remodeling, but not until engineers declared the White House structurally unsound and in need of a new framework.

In the midst of this constant change and upheaval, the White House's dual role as creator and preserver of history has never been lost on its inhabitants. Mrs. Calvin Coolidge was particularly insistent that this role be recognized. She convinced Congress to pass a resolution allowing the White House to accept gifts of suitable antiques—actual pieces and replicas of the furniture of past presidents. Since that time, many first ladies have made it a personal crusade to find and restore furniture and other household objects from the White House's past. As Jacqueline Kennedy remarked as she set about restoring the rooms of her new home,

"Everything in the White House must have a reason for being there."

This commitment to the history and heritage of the White House is not surprising. It must be both a proud and intensely humbling experience to set up residence in this grand old home. Under this one roof some of our greatest leaders have played out the most memorable and significant scenes of our history. Twenty-sixth president Theodore Roosevelt was inspired in his work by the specter of another great leader, Abraham Lincoln. "I think of Lincoln," he said, "shambling, homely, with his strong, sad, deeply furrowed face, all the time. I see him in the different rooms and in the halls." And as Lincoln inspired Roosevelt, so might Roosevelt's presence—felt in the furniture he chose for his bedroom or the paintings he hung on his walls or the words of his letters and papers—inspire a future leader. It is impossible for a man or a woman to walk the halls of this house and remain unaware of the great continuity of the American experience.

The White House is open free of charge to all visitors. Tours usually include a visit to the Library, the East Room, and the Green, Blue, and Red Rooms. The East Room is the "Public Audience Chamber," the scene of concerts and recitals for visiting dignitaries. More comprehensive tours can be arranged through members of Congress well in advance of the visit.

One of the most identifiable rooms in the White House is not on public display—the president's Oval Office. From this office —illuminated by the sunlight that pours through large windows overlooking the Rose Garden and decorated by the president's own family photographs and personal mementos—American presidents speak to the people they serve. It is here that they bear the burdens and the joys of office, and here that the true significance of the White House is most apparent. As American citizens, we must all echo the prayer of John Adams that only the "honest and wise" serve here, for it is in this office, within this fine and storied old American home, that the course of our country is charted.

Spicy Corn and Black Bean Salad

2   11-ounce cans whole kernel sweet corn
      with red and green sweet peppers, rinsed and drained
1   15-ounce can black beans, rinsed and drained
½   cup sliced fresh mushrooms
½   cup chopped green onions
½   cup thinly sliced cucumbers
2   tablespoons finely chopped fresh
      jalapeño pepper (optional)
½   cup olive or vegetable oil
¼   cup rice wine vinegar or white cider vinegar
¼   cup orange juice
1   clove garlic, minced
½   teaspoon salt
¼   cup freshly chopped cilantro
1   tablespoon grated orange peel
1 to 2   teaspoons cumin seed (optional)
      Fresh lettuce leaves

In 2-quart mixing bowl, combine first six ingredients; stir to mix well.

Combine oil, vinegar, orange juice, and garlic in a jar with a lid and shake well. Pour dressing over salad and toss gently. Cover and refrigerate 1 to 2 hours or until ready to serve.

Just before serving, drain salad. Add cilantro, orange peel, and cumin, if desired. Serve in lettuce-lined bowl or in individual lettuce cups. Can be refrigerated for several days. Makes about 1½ quarts salad.

Louis Comfort Tiffany

In homes throughout America, the Tiffany lamp not only brightens rooms, but, with its vibrant mosaics of colored glass, adds a touch of simple beauty to the scenes of everyday life. This is a fitting legacy to the lamp's creator, Louis Comfort Tiffany, an artist who devoted his life to providing Americans with "good art in our homes."

Tiffany was born in 1848 to Harriet and Charles Tiffany, head of the successful silver and jewelry firm Tiffany and Company. Louis was the Tiffanys' oldest son, but although it was assumed he would eventually take over his father's business, he was uninspired both by the business world and by his role as presumptive heir. In 1866, only eighteen years old, Louis announced his intention to pursue a career in art. For the next three years he studied painting in Paris.

Just as he was unable to conform to the demands of the family business, however, Louis found himself stifled by the world of the fine arts, a world that he believed valued technique over true artistic expression and that cared more about impressing the community of artists than reaching the general public. Tiffany had been experimenting with blown glass, and as his dissatisfaction with the fine arts grew, his interest in the decorative and applied arts blossomed. Eventually, he founded Louis Comfort Tiffany and Associated Artists and began a career as a decorator.

Within years, Tiffany had gained a reputation as America's foremost decorator. It was no surprise, therefore, that when the country's most prestigious home needed redecorating, Tiffany was entrusted with the job. Chester A. Arthur, recently elected president, declared that he would not move into the White House until it was cleaned and redecorated. He also declared money no object and promised that what the government would not pay, he would. Arthur personally chose Tiffany for the job.

Over seven weeks during the winter of 1882-1883, at a cost of over $15,000, Tiffany and Associates brought new life to the presidential home, redecorating in their distinctive style the Corridor, the East Room, the State Dining Room, and the Red and Blue Parlors. Each room was a remarkable achievement, but the East Room was a showcase. The ceiling was finished in gold and ivory and a many-hued opalescent glass screen rose from the floor between stately pillars, separating the corridor from the vestibule. The screen was designed both for its aesthetic value and for the practical purpose of providing privacy for the president's family. (Unfortunately, Tiffany's vision was not universally acclaimed. In 1904, President Theodore Roosevelt ordered the screen broken "in small pieces" and discarded. The screen was later replaced at a cost of $15,000.)

With the decoration of the White House, Tiffany's art became a part of the most prestigious home in America. His most lasting achievement, however, would come on a scale less grand—the typical American home. The Tiffany lamp, first sold in 1895, was the medium Tiffany had searched for throughout his career. Fashioned from beautifully colored and shaped iridescent glass, the lamps transformed common domestic objects into wonderful works of art, and in the process, guaranteed Louis Tiffany a place in American art history.

Tiffany was a true innovator, revolutionizing the techniques of glasswork and bringing a new level of respect to the applied and decorative arts. Along with lamps, Tiffany and his company produced desk sets, ash trays, tableware, and other objects for the home; and working with artists such as Maxfield Parish, Tiffany created exquisite stained glass windows which can be seen today in some of our most beautiful churches and most prestigious museums.

Throughout his life, Louis Tiffany sought to create beauty, rejecting imitative forms and taking his inspiration from the rich and varied color and form of nature. He dreamed that one day America would be an important center of the arts and that art would be a central part of everyday American life. And while the Tiffany lamp and its many imitations may never be classified as masterpieces of fine art, they may very well have a more profound and universal influence than any painting ever could. Working with household objects, Tiffany brought his art to the people, not by way of museums, but directly into their own homes.

MY HOME

Ruth Glidden

My home must be a sunny place,
A place up high,
Where the sky can bring
Soft birds to nest and sing
A treasured while,
Where God's sweet grace
Can rest and smile,
And hope take wing;

My home must be a shield
From wind and storm,
Where tired folk
May rest and warm
Their hearts and weary feet,
Where sun and sky
And bird and man
And God's sweet grace
Can rest and meet.

MILLBRIDGE, MAINE
Dietrich Stock Photos, Inc.

Our House

I like to see a lovely lawn
Bediamoned with dew at dawn,
But mine is often trampled bare,
Because the youngsters gather there.

I like a spotless house and clean
Where many a touch of grace is seen,
But mine is often tossed about
By youngsters racing in and out.

I like a quiet house at night
Where I may sit to read and write,
But my peace flies before the tones
Of three brass throated saxophones.

My books to tumult are resigned,
In vain my furniture is shined,
My lawn is bare, my flowers fall,
Youth rides triumphant over all.

I love the grass, I love the rose,
And every living thing that grows.
I love the books I ponder o'er,
But, oh, I love the children more!

And so unto myself I say:
Be mine the house where youngsters play.
Oh, little girl, oh, healthy boy,
Be mine the house which you enjoy!

Bed in Summer

Robert Louis Stevenson

In winter I get up at night
And dress by yellow candlelight.
In summer, quite the other way,
I have to go to bed by day.

I have to go to bed and see
The birds still hopping on the tree,
Or hear the grown-up people's feet
Still going past me on the street.

And does it not seem hard to you,
When all the sky is clear and blue,
And I should like so much to play,
I have to go to bed by day?

Northwestern University students show their support of the war effort by wearing cotton stockings instead of silk.

UPI/Bettmann Photos

Silk Shutdown

After a week of uncertainty, the American silk industry was told last Friday by the OPM that when the existing three week supply of processed silk is used up no more raw silk can be processed without the authorization of the Director of Priorities. Fabricators had about a four month supply of raw silk in sight, but the Army and Navy declared these stocks represented the minimum required during the next two years

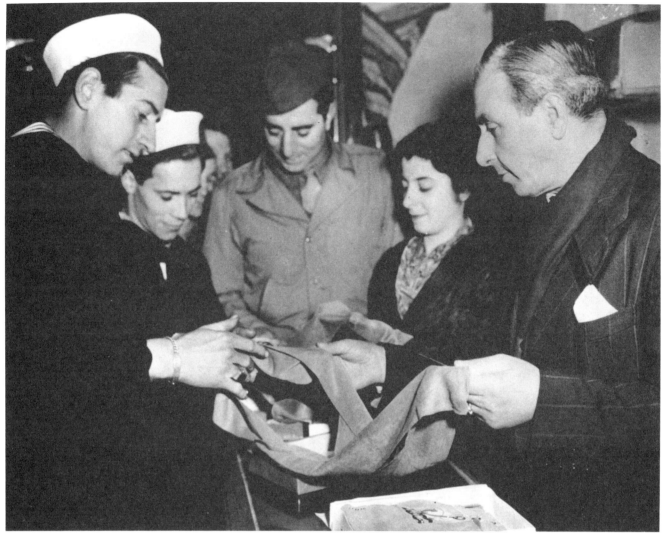

Three U. S. servicemen stock up on silk stocking in Naples, Italy.

for parachutes and powder bags, although synthetic and cotton-yarn substitutes respectively are reported satisfactory for each. Unless the Administration decides to admit more silk from Japan, most of the workers in hosiery, necktie, and underwear mills may soon be out of work. In any case, the order brought the war home to the public with a smash by threatening the supply of silk stockings, the American woman's most characteristic article of clothing, which is consumed at an annual rate of 47,000,000 dozen pairs.

All last week hosiery sales were heavy everywhere as the ladies prepared for the worst. Meanwhile, government officials anxiously conferred with the silk industry and labor leaders on plans to soften the economic blow.

One possibility is that women may have to turn to cotton stockings, though they unanimously snubbed a new sheer, mercerized lisle hose hopefully introduced last year. Other rumored developments include the wide adoption of the collegiate bare-legged fad, painting of legs and, to the distress of many men, longer skirts.

HOUSES

Annabelle Attwater

When we give up a house we love, I find

That even as children we can't let go,

For somewhere in the fringes of our mind

There clings a door, a stair, a portico:

In one large house with windows high and clear

I watch for love as when but seventeen;

The house where I was wed, how very dear,

The tall porch pillars, the great door between;

The duplex where he took me as a bride,

The old high chair, the playpen by the bed.

Homes, old and new, I learn when I depart

I leave with each a portion of my heart.

I Like a House

June Masters Bacher

I like a house that shows its age,
Whose wrinkled forehead wall
Supports the trees that slowly grow
And lean for fear they'll fall
Against a darkened shingle roof,
Most often spread with leaves
And scalloped with the swinging nests
Of swallows in the eaves.

I like a house that somehow holds
The echo of a song
That neighbors stop and listen to
Then take its notes along.
No architect can build this house;
Kind hearts design its plan
And lines come from its character
Of being friend to man.

An Old House

Marel Brown

They set this house upon a sturdy hill
And built its pillars firm of native stone.
Its timbers seasoned with the years until
The strength of time became its very own.
The roof is weathered with the rain and sun
And through its doors the winds of peace
    have blown.
Brave hearts have fought grim battles
    here and won;
Their valiant courage like a mantle falls
Upon this house. Old-fashioned roses run
Their fragrant fingers up the aging walls
To bless the lives of those who now
    abide in love
And walk contented through its halls.
Was time or stone or love that never dies
The source from which your charm has
    been supplied?

CRAFTWORKS

Photo Transfers:
A Simple Way to Show Off Favorite Family Photos

Turn favorite photographs into washable fabric designs to wear, carry, or share! Without harming your photographs, this simple photo transfer method allows you to show off a cherished child or grandchild, share a moment from the past, or enjoy a special occasion again and again.

Materials Needed

Photocopy of photograph (*Note*: Photocopies can be obtained from libraries, small printers, or some grocery stores and usually cost less than a quarter. Do not use original photos for this process.)

Photo transfer medium (available at craft and hobby stores)

Fabric (T-shirt, sweatshirt, canvas tote bag, etc.)

1-inch sponge brush

Scissors, rolling pin, heavy cardboard, wax paper, plastic wrap, sponge scrubber, pins or tape, fabric markers or fabric paint (optional)

Select Photograph

For a black and white transfer, use either a color or black and white photo and make a black and white photocopy. For a full-color transfer, use a color photo and make a color photocopy. The transfer method will reverse the image, so avoid photos with any letters or numbers.

Prepare Fabric

Select a fabric with a smooth texture. Cottons and poly-cotton blends work well. Pre-wash the fabric to remove all the sizing and to pre-shrink. (Do not use fabric softeners or dryer sheets during this step as they will affect the transfer.)

With pins or tape, secure fabric to a piece of heavy cardboard covered with plastic wrap. This provides a firm working surface and prevents the transfer medium from soaking through.

Apply Transfer

Trim the photocopy so that only desired image remains and place it face up on a piece of wax paper. Using a sponge brush, spread the transfer medium evenly over the face of the photocopy, about $1/16$-to $1/8$-inch deep. Place the photocopy, transfer medium side down, onto the fabric. With very light pressure, use a rolling pin to smooth the photocopy onto the fabric, removing air bubbles. With a damp cloth, remove excess medium from sides of transfer. Let dry flat for twenty-four hours.

Remove Transfer

Remove fabric from cardboard and flood entire transfer area with water. Wait five minutes; then, with your finger, begin rolling the wet paper out from the center of the transfer. Continue to work from the center to the edges, using a sponge scrubber or a "scrubber" fabric painting brush to remove the remaining paper fuzz. Allow the transfer to dry completely. Repeat until no paper remains.

When all paper has been removed and the fabric is dry, wet the transfer with your sponge brush and spread three to four drops of transfer medium evenly over the transfer area to seal for long wear.

Finishing

After drying thoroughly, items are ready for any extra details. Use fabric markers or fabric paint to add borders, lettering, or design.

Care Instructions

To wash, turn garment inside-out and machine wash on gentle cycle in cool water. Machine dry on low setting. Iron, if necessary, using a press cloth.

Marty Sowder Brooks demonstrates her crafts weekly on a Nashville, Tennessee, television talk show. She lives in Madison, Tennessee, with her husband.

Photo by Gerald Koser

FROM MY
G·A·R·D·E·N
JOURNAL

Deana Deck

Low-Maintenance Gardening

The true gardeners of the world—those who look forward to quiet hours of nurturing and who treasure the beauty that springs from their care—know a calmness of spirit and a sense of accomplishment unlike any other. For these people, the limitations of advancing age and decreasing strength that make the cherished tasks of gardening painful or impossible are a source of great frustration.

Is there a way to hold on to the garden even when it is necessary to give up most of the gardening? Yes, with some advance planning and an understanding of the three basics of low-maintenance gardening: ground covers, perennials, and mulch.

Ground covers cut down on mowing, fertilizing, seeding, and weeding; they also create a beautiful landscape that can be enjoyed year round with little maintenance. Ground covers are the most versatile of the low-maintenance plants. The most common are English ivy and its cousins for full sun situations, and *vinca minor* for shady spots. There are many other choices, however, like Ajuga, ferns, Dutch clover, or even mosses.

In temperate climates, honeysuckle—usually thought of as something draped across backyard fences—is an excellent, fast-growing ground cover. The Henry variety of honeysuckle is an easily contained vine and is evergreen except in cases of extremely cold winters. *Lirope,* or lilyturf, is excellent for edging paved areas and walkways or for lush plantings in large shaded areas, although it does equally well in bright light.

Few ground covers have as many attributes, however, as the prostrate junipers, most of which are hardy to -25°. Foliage choices vary from the silvery "Blue Rug" variety to the gray-green "Bar Harbor," which turns a silvery plum in winter.

Perennials are the second element in a care-free garden. In this category are not only the herbaceous rooted varieties, but also plants that grow from bulbs, rhizomes, and tubers—in short, anything that you plant and forget, but can expect to see blooming merrily away in your garden year after year. In this group are daffodils and day lilies, crocuses and hyacinths, irises, daisies, peonies, hollyhocks, and lilies.

Plant the daffodils and Narcissus among the ground covers. They will appear and bloom right on schedule each year, and the job of disguising their wilting, yellow foliage each year will be taken over by the ground cover.

Among the perennials, place a few self-seeding annuals, such as *Cleome*, cosmos, and *Coreopsis*. Any plant that grows wild in your area is also a good choice. Remember all those daisies and black-eyed Susans growing along the roadside? Nobody goes out there to feed and water them; obviously, they are the sort of no-work flower you want in your garden.

Mulch is the third element. If you mulch deeply—six to eight inches at least—you won't have to weed, you won't have to fertilize more than once a year, and you'll seldom have to replace plants lost to cold, drought, or disease.

The most important element in a low-maintenance garden is planning. A well-laid plan eliminates much of the hard work associated with landscaping and gardening. Start by finding out what climate zone you live in and selecting only plants for that zone. Plan on enriching your soil to a depth of about eighteen inches before planting so that the garden can sustain life with a minimum of work. Do your research and decide which elements of your garden or landscape are most important.

The switch to a low-maintenance garden can be either a complete overhaul or a gradual trend, depending upon your own needs and limitations. But whatever those limitations, take comfort in the knowledge that the garden is flexible, and the relaxation and peace of mind it provides are not necessarily tied to endless hours of backbreaking work.

Deana Deck lives in Nashville, Tennessee, where her garden column is a regular feature in the Tennessean.

Photo Overleaf
FRENCH RIVER
Prince Edward Island, Canada
Gene Ahrens, Photographer

The House by the Side of the Road

Sam Walter Foss

There are hermit souls that live withdrawn
In the place of their self-content;
There are souls like stars, that dwell apart,
In a fellowless firmament;
There are pioneer souls that blaze their paths
Where highways never ran—
But let me live by the side of the road
And be a friend to man.

Let me live in a house by the side of the road,
Where the race of men go by—
The men who are good and the men who are bad,
As good and bad as I.
I would not sit in the scorner's seat,
Or hurl the cynic's ban—
Let me live in a house by the side of the road
And be a friend to man.

I see from my house by the side of the road,
By the side of the highway of life,
The men who press with the ardor of hope,
The men who are faint with the strife.
But I turn not away from their smiles nor their tears,
Both parts of an infinite plan—
Let me live in a house by the side of the road
And be a friend to man.

I know there are brook-gladdened meadows ahead,
And mountains of wearisome height;
That the road passes on through the long afternoon
And stretches away to the night.
But still I rejoice when the travelers rejoice,
And weep with the strangers that moan,
Nor live in my house by the side of the road
Like a man who dwells alone.

Let me live in my house by the side of the road,
It's here the race of men go by—
They are good, they are bad, they are weak, they are strong,
Wise, foolish—so am I;
Then why should I sit in the scorner's seat,
Or hurl the cynic's ban?
Let me live in my house by the side of the road
And be a friend to man.

My Hometown

Craig E. Sathoff

When I return,
The main street still is filled
With pleasant faces and glad hellos,
With an atmosphere of calm,
With time for neighborly concern,
With joy in sharing another's fortune
Or heartfelt words to one who mourns.

Hometown is more than just a town;
It is a way of life, a place of
Peace and quiet, and when I return
It is as if I have never been gone;
And in my heart I have not.

Photo Opposite
CROSSROADS HAMLET
York County, Pennsylvania
Grant Heilman Photography

Old Towns

Josephine Powell Beaty

The artistry of age is here
In ivied brick and mellowed stone.
Tall trees their slanting shadows cast
Across the well-worn gravelled walks
Whose rustled gates have ceased to guard
And hang on limping hinge ajar,
Inviting idle trespassers.
Old houses sun themselves and muse
On other manners, days, and ways,
And faces seen no more that fill
The yellowing leaves of memory's book.

My Town

Helen Virden

This town is mine.
It fits me like an easy chair,
As comfortable.
I know each wrinkle,
The sturdiness of arms,
The softness of each cushion
And where a spring, half-worn,
Must be avoided.
Its contours fit;
We have molded each to the other.
This is my town.

Proof Enough

Jessie Cannon Eldridge

On a summer day I find
Proof enough for all mankind
Of God's glory everywhere . . .
Honeysuckle in the air,
Violets and dew-kissed roses,
Gold bees honeying their noses,
Pleated daisies, quilted clover,
Blue slate swallows soaring over,
Flowered apple trees aglow,
Aspens leaning in a row,
Wrinkled elm trees in a line,
Speckled birch and needled pine,
Fertile gardens, fields of wheat,
Velvet grass grown at my feet . . .
All things lovely, all things fair—
Proof of God's love everywhere.

SUNFLOWER FIELD
Door County, Wisconsin
Gene Ahrens, Photographer

CHRONICLE
— Lansing Christman —

Give me a plot of ground in the hill country, where I can walk out in the fields and meadows, where I can follow a meandering stream through pastures and wood-lands, by marshes and bogs; there I will be at home.

There is nothing more I need, for I find my treasures in wild pastures with their field spar-

rows and meadow larks, and the blossoms of morning glory and Queen Anne's lace. My wealth may be found in old woodlands, with their woodpeckers, thrushes, and owls, their deer and their squirrels. There are riches in brushlands and thickets where trumpet vine crawls and creeps and climbs, where the wild Clematis grows and rabbits hide.

I cherish common things. As my footsteps lead me away from the beaten paths I listen to the sermons along the way and I find comfort and inspiration. I find fulfillment in the rural wayside—in the loveliness of a flower or a weed, in the intricacy of a lichen, in the elegance of a stately tree, and in the artistry of a stone. I am at home among such things.

The author of two published books, Lansing Christman has been contributing to Ideals *for almost twenty years. Mr. Christman has also been published in several American, foreign, and braille anthologies. He lives in rural South Carolina.*

VACATION

John E. Vance

The hills and valleys
Long ago adopted me;
The persimmons and wild strawberries
Were better than manna or candy.
Hickory smoke seasoned me;
Songs of birds along the wild trails
Were like celestial music.
I have been browned by the sun
And cooled by rain and snow,

Now I need a vacation
From concrete and steel,
From days punched out
On timecards.
From inside cages
To outside vastness
I need to go;
Where men have not left
Their trademarks,
So that my fingertips
Can touch the sky;
Then I will be at peace and free
And feel in close harmony
With my creator.

Photo Opposite
CALIFORNIA DAISIES
Stone Lagoon
Redwood National Park
Crescent City, California

Earth, My Village

Eloise Hamilton

The earth, my village, lifts its steepled heights
Of mountains like a granite worship call,
And down the little valleys of my mind
Rings the clear summons of a waterfall.

And every roof is home, and every path
Familiar; each wanderer I meet
My brother, friend, a pilgrim, just as I,
Passing but once along a village street.

Counterpart

Mildred Morris Gilbert

Today beside a mountain lake
I paused and watched the sunlight make
Reflections of the peaks and pines
Intricately laced with lines
Of twofold beauty, and my soul
Exalted. Resting on a knoll,
Inspired, I said a little prayer
And saw God's presence mirrored there.

Adventure

Beatrice Wheeler

Today I spied a winding path
That beckoned me to come;
I followed it with eager steps
And soon was far from home.
I passed a squirrel on his perch;
He chattered loudly at me.
I saw a timid rabbit run
To hide behind a tree.
I nodded to a happy flower;
I chased a butterfly;
I sat beside a murmuring stream
And flung wee pebbles high.
I saw a spider spin her lace
And stopped a while to view
The landscape from a wooded hill
And see the sky of blue.
I lingered 'neath the whispering pine
And thought how good was He
Who placed such beauty on this earth
That mortals here might see.

Photo Opposite
MIDDLE NORTH FALLS
Silver Falls State Park
Oregon
Dietrich Stock Photos

SEA SPELL

Rose Koralewsky

Ah, what a glorious symphony
Of sun and sky and sea!
The slumberous murmur on the shore
Of blue waves spent, the journey o'er;
The breath of salt air, cool and keen,
Stirring the beach-grass glaucous green;
The gulls' parabolas of flight,

Long sweeping strokes of silver light;
The golden fervor of the sun,
By soul and body felt as one—
They cast on us an age-old spell;
We lie entranced; and none can tell,
When ends the dream-like summer day,
How passed the enchanted hours away.

HOMECOMING

Hal Borland

More than half the pleasure of going is in the return, as any traveler knows. To go, to see the far place, the place beyond the horizon, is exciting; but to return is satisfying as few other things can ever be. To know after absence the familiar street and road and village and house is to know again the satisfaction of home.

Few of us are that kind of traveler who can be at home forever away from home. The new, the strange, and the different have their lure, but one needs a place to call his own. One needs to belong somewhere, to feel the roots, however tenuous, of identity with place. Home, we call it, whether it be a room or a house or an apartment, a farm or a plot of grass or a well-known street or park. Home, where one can feel and touch and see and find comfort in familiar things. The place where one belongs.

Man, being man and an ambulatory creature with a degree of restlessness in his blood, must be up and gone from time to time. He must go, if only to assure himself that the horizon has no boundary. He must move from here to yonder, if only to know that he is neither slave nor prisoner. What are hills for, if not to have a farther side? And what is the purpose of that distant rim of sky if not to lure a man beyond his own small orbit? But once one has gone, one must come back.

And that is the final satisfaction of a trip, whether it is a vacation or just a journey—the return itself. The homecoming. The trip back, and the home at the end. To go is good, but to come back is best.

BITS & PIECES

There is a magic in that little word, home; it is a mystic circle that surrounds comforts and virtues never known beyond its hallowed limits.

Robert Southey

It was the policy of the good old gentleman to make his children feel that home was the happiest place in the world; and I value this delicious home feeling as one of the choicest gifts a parent can bestow.

Washington Irving

Peace and rest at length have come,
All the day's long toil is past;
And each heart is whispering,
"Home, Home at last!"

Thomas Hood

66

Home is the resort of love, of joy, of peace, and plenty, where supporting and supported, polished friends and dearest relatives mingle in bliss.

James Thomson

A man travels the world over in search of what he needs and returns home to find it.

George Moore

Our home joys are the most delightful earth affords, and the joy of parents in their children is the most holy joy of humanity. It makes their hearts pure and good, it lifts men up to their Father in heaven.

Johann Pestolazzi

If God has taught us all truth in teaching us to love, then he has given us an interpretation of our whole duty to our households. We are not born as the partridge in the wood, or the ostrich of the desert, to be scattered everywhere; but we are to be grouped together, and brooded by love, and reared day by day in that first of churches, the family.

Henry Ward Beecher

Enduring Things

Mary E. Linton

And what, then,
  is the all-important goal
To which we drive ourselves
  and have no time
To listen to the singing of the soul,
Or rise on spirit's wings
  to thoughts sublime?
One day the world will grind
  much as before
Without our grim direction,
  and the wheels
Will somehow turn
  when we have passed the door
That leads beyond four walls
  and three square meals.
And what then will we have to take along
Where there are neither pockets,
  vaults nor shelves,
When all that we can hold
  will be our song
And what we worked to build
  into ourselves?

Oh, listen to the universe that sings
Through hearts attuned
  to Life's enduring things.

LOW TIDE
Annisquam Light
Massachusetts
Gene Ahrens, Photographer

Coming Home

Elisabeth Weaver Winstead

The beloved homeplace was waiting,
In tranquil, quiet welcome it stood—
Beckoning home of childhood days
At the end of the sheltering wood.

The handsome, stout, fieldstone chimney,
Silent sentinel, stood proud and serene;
Solid wood of burnished oak timbers
Formed sturdy walls and strong beams.

Bright sun-glow softened each doorway
And lent enchanting grace,

To time-wrapped enduring splendor
In this nostalgic place.

Swarms of honeybees gathered
Where star-shine daisies sweep,
Beneath fruit-laden apple trees
Whose roots stretched long and deep.

Shy squirrels ran in the woodland;
Wild berries, chestnuts, and grouse
Still stayed in lavish abundance
Around the sweet, cherished old house.

The matted, thick brookside grasses
In fragrant, white-flowered bouquets
Held within tall windswept thatches
Mingled memories of dear, golden days.

The Open Door

Elizabeth Olsen

Ever an open door
To house, to heart,
To warmth and ease;

No bolt, no lock,
The only key a need
Of understanding.

Those who enter there
Find love, in turn
Give life and cheer.

A fair exchange, a gift
Of each to each, comes
Through an open door.

72

Photo Opposite
BUCKLEPEAT BED AND BREAKFAST
Hawkshead, England
Dietrich Stock Photos

THROUGH MY WINDOW
Pamela Kennedy

Sarah's Rocker Speaks

I was delivered to the family in 1918, a gift from Charles to Sarah on the occasion of their first wedding anniversary. He ordered me from the Sears Roebuck Catalogue, Number 1R346:

"A beautiful rocker of the latest pattern. Large and comfortable, with a high paneled back richly carved. Made of the best seasoned and selected quarter sawed golden oak, elegantly finished, making a rocker that will be an ornament to any room. Our special price—$3.45."

It was a lavish gift, but Charles said, "It will be the beginning of our home—something store-bought and new."

Sarah lovingly placed me beside the wood-burning stove and rocked in me every evening after supper. She was knitting booties then, for her firstborn, and she hummed as the needles clicked together in syncopated rhythm.

By fall, when the baby had arrived, we rocked together even more—in the middle of the night, at noon, after supper. She sang to him then, lullabies and nursery rhymes and favorite old hymns. I loved the songs, and we moved in time to her soft alto melodies.

Seasons turned and months flew by and the little one grew. Now he stood as she rocked him, bouncing in time to her singing, chewing with newly cut teeth on my back and arms. There were grooves in my fine finish and scars on my polished curves, but I didn't mind. They were a part of the family's life, a testimony to the home.

74

Two more little boys followed the first, and all were rocked to sleep in my sturdy oak embrace. Sarah and I comforted them when knees were skinned or elbows banged, or when bruised egos needed mending.

In the summer I was often dragged to the broad front porch. There we'd sit, Sarah and I, watching the children play in the orchard under the gnarled cherry trees as she shelled peas or peeled apples. She was a queen, my Sarah, enthroned on oak, surveying the rich kingdom before her.

Sometimes, in the evening, she would sit still by the stove, mending socks or turning a hem as she listened to one of the boys recite the state capitals or multiplication tables to the rhythm of my familiar creaking.

The boys grew strong and tall and put away baseball bats and butterfly nets. They stacked their school books on the shelf and found other jobs, "men's work" they called it. Then, one by one, letters came, calling them to war. One went to Europe, two to the Pacific, leaving Charlie, Sarah, and me at home.

Late at night, Sarah still sat by the firelight, reading their mail over and over. Again we rocked together as she tried to read between the lines, willing them safely home. Her knitting needles clicked rapidly, making sweaters and woolen stockings for other mothers' sons.

We were there together in the parlor rocking when the eldest returned. "I pictured you there just like that, Ma," he said, "sitting in your old rocker, waiting. It kept me going."

The others came back too, miraculously, and Sarah sat, surrounded by her sons once more. She rocked and smiled and listened to their stories of places she would never see: Mindanao, Buna Beach, Normandy.

When the boys went off again, it was for love, not war; they left to begin homes and families of their own. "Come back often!" Sarah told them, "You are always welcome here." And things were once again as they had been at first—Charlie, Sarah, and me.

We stayed in the old house, but the empty rooms and creaking stairs cried out for children's feet and voices. "I suppose we ought to move," Charlie said one day. Sarah looked around and nodded slowly in agreement, adding, "It would be less to keep up, don't you think?"

The decision was made; the house was sold and the furniture given away. "I'd like to keep the rocker," Sarah said quietly. She ran her fingers over the scraped places, the mended back, and the teething scars. "It'll remind me of our home."

Charlie smiled and kissed her cheek. "Fifty years this spring," he said with pride.

Now I rock on newer floors in smaller, modern rooms; but Sarah still hums the old songs. And the knitting needles still click together, making booties for great grandsons. The children visit often, all loudly clamoring for a turn in "Grammy's chair." I do not mind their raucous play, but when they leave, the quiet is a comfort. Then Sarah comes and we pick up our well-established harmony of wood and song that softly whispers "home."

Pamela Kennedy is a freelance writer of short stories, articles, essays, and children's books. Mother of three children, she is married to a naval officer and has made her home on both U.S. coasts. She currently resides in Hawaii and draws her material from her own experiences and memories, adding bits of imagination to create a story or mood.

So Long as There Are Homes

Grace Noll Crowell

So long as there are homes to which men turn
　　at close of day;
So long as there are homes where children are,
　　where women stay—
If love and loyalty and faith be found
　　across those sills—
A stricken nation can recover from
　　its gravest ills.

So long as there are homes where fires burn
　　and there is bread;
So long as there are homes where lamps are lit
　　and prayers said;
Although people falter through the dark
　　and nations grope—
With God himself back of these little homes—
　　we still can hope.

Home

Phyllis Michael

May our home
Be a haven
Of peace
And contentment,
Knowing laughter
And love
Without strife;

May our home
Be a harbor
Where we find
New courage
To sail the sea
Of life.

Prayer for Today

Hilda Butler Farr

I only ask
That home shall be
A place where loved ones
Come to rest;
Where peace abides
And faith exists
Somehow because
I did my best.
Tomorrow—
It may never come—
And consequently I do pray
That I may have
Enough of strength
To serve the ones
I love today.

AN OPPORTUNITY TO COMPLETE YOUR COLLECTION OF *IDEALS* MAGAZINE!

Here is your once-a-year opportunity to complete your collection of the beautiful and seasonal *Ideals!* Many of our readers request particular issues, but only a few of a limited number of issues are available. Order now, either by phone and credit card, or send us a check at the special price of $3.50 for each book ordered. We will pay postage.

I10540A Autumn 1987
Brilliant photography from the most beautiful season of the year, "Hearty Autumn Soups," "The Last Leaf" by Pam Kennedy, and "Country Chronicle" goes in search of hickory nuts.

I10567A Christmas 1987
"Home for Christmas" by Laura Ingalls Wilder, "A Winter Walk" by Henry Thoreau, recipes for German Stollen and Holiday Wreath Pie, "The Second Christmas" by Pam Kennedy, and spectacular photos of the season.

I10591A Valentine 1988
"Sawdust and Dreams" by Edgar A. Guest, Collector's Corner on Old-Fashioned Valentines, directions for making heart sachets and garlands, and, "An American Valentine" by Pam Kennedy.

I10605A Easter 1988
Collector's Corner features bisque and china dolls, directions for making an applique Bible cover, "He Is Risen Indeed" by Pam Kennedy, and "Relics of an Old World Easter" by Walter Wentz.

I10613A Mother's Day 1988
"A Thousand Million Questions" by Phyllis Michael, "Once a Mother, Always a Mother" by Pam Kennedy, "Mother's Day" by Edgar A. Guest, and directions for making Applique Rose Pillows.

I10621A Summertime 1988
Collector's Corner looks at old postcards, make rose potpourri from backyard roses, "Salute to the Statue of Liberty," applique a barbecue apron, and gorgeous scenery from around the nation.

I10648A Autumn 1988
Opening spread is the beautiful "Birches" by Robert Frost, Collector's Corner features old U.S. coins, recipes for autumn casseroles, Pam Kennedy's "Reflections," and directions for a cross-stitch glass case.

I10656A Thanksgiving 1988
"A Time for Settling In" by Carol McCray, applique a Pilgrim potholder, Collector's Corner looks at antique clocks, and Pam Kennedy's "A Letter Home" from a might-have-been adventurer.

I10664A Christmas 1988
"Keeping Christmas" by Henry Van Dyke, "The Twenty-Sixth of December" by Donald Stoltz, directions for Patchwork Stockings, Collector's Corner featuring Electric Trains, The Story of the Birth of Christ from Luke 2, and the beauty of the season in photography.

I10699A Valentine 1989
Featuring articles on "Phoenix Bird" pattern china, "Down Life's Stream" by Margaret Sangster, Craftworks featuring Decoupage, and love poetry befitting the season.

I10702A Easter 1989
The religious Easter Story, directions for decorative sugar eggs, Pam Kennedy's fictional account of Simon meeting the Messiah, Collector's Corner featuring miniatures, and breathtaking photos of the flowers of spring.

I10737A Mother's Day 1989
Norman Rockwell's Collectibles are featured, the planting and care of lilacs discussed, "My Cinderella Grandmother" by Kathleen Gilbert, recipes for strawberry torte and other delights,

I10753A Home 1989
Garden Journal shows you how to plant a "Cutting Garden," "Country Chronicle" takes a walk and listens to the sounds of the countryside, directions for applique sweatshirts, and "Martha's Home" by Cynthia Wyatt.

I1077XA Thanksgiving 1989
Features the history and the beauty of the season for the whole family, grow a sweet potato houseplant, "Let's Be Thankful" by Mary Reiter, "The First Feast" by Jane Austin, and "Giving Thanks" by Joy Ward.

I10788A Christmas 1989
Directions for making felt ornaments for the tree, "A Stable Boy's Christmas" by Pam Kennedy, "Luke, the Man Who Gave Us Christmas," "Christmas in America" by Angela Hunt, and "Let Us Keep Christmas" by Grace Noll Crowell.

I1080XA Valentine 1990
Roses and love poetry, how to grow African violets, antique purses, how to make candle holder skirts, and Pam Kennedy on Valentines from God

I10818A Easter 1990
Ten pages of the story of Christ's death and resurrection illustrated with the "Old Master" paintings of Carl Heinrich Bloch; Pam Kennedy's "The Centurion's Story;" and how to make an Easter wreath for the door.

I10826A Mother's Day 1990
Learn all about "Mothersense," cameos, growing roses, and when nylon stockings were new. Travel to "Dixieland," home of Thomas Wolfe, who said "You can't go home again."

I10834A Country 1990
Poems on the loveliness of the country and nature; how to make throw pillows from old neckties; and collecting antique butter molds. Some of the prettiest photos ever.

I10842A Home 1990
Poems about home, houses, and families; read about gardens and view their beauty; learn how to plant a cutting garden; and collecting antique flatirons.

I10850A Friendship 1990
Poems on friends and the end of summer; learn how some collect ancestors for their family trees; Pam Kennedy's "Friends;" directions for cross-stitching a basket liner for the new neighbor.

I10869A Thanksgiving 1990
Poems and prose of thanksgiving, preparations for winter, photos of the splendor of nature at autumn, and poems of the harvest; learn about Nathaniel Hawthorne and visit Salem, Massachusetts

I10877A Christmas 1990
Filled with joy, from the story of Christ's birth illustrated by beautiful, traditional paintings, to how to keep a poinsettia all year, to gifts to make from the kitchen and beautiful, painted sweatshirts, this is a wonderful issue